Silly Dreamers

Matt Sims

D0067618

High Noon Books
Novato, California

Cover Illustration: Ralph Voltz
Interior Illustrations: Kevin at KJA-Artists

Copyright © 2015, 2004, by High Noon Books, 20 Leveroni Court, Novato, CA 94949-5746. All rights reserved. Printed in the United States of America. No part of this publication may be reproduced, stored in a retrieval system, or transmitted, in any form or by any means, electronic, mechanical photocopying, recording or otherwise, without the prior written permission of the publisher.

International Standard Book Number:
978-1-57128-362-7

24 23 22 21 20 19 18 17 16
10 09 08 07 06 05 04 03 02
2015 edition

www.HighNoonBooks.com

Sound Out Set C-1 order #8313-7

Contents

The Perfect Job

"I'm really happy your dad could get us these jobs," Leroy stated. He leaned over to empty a waste basket under a metal desk.

"Me, too," Jason agreed. "It's a snap

cleaning these rooms. Besides, we can play music all we want." Jason heaved a sweeper across the thick carpet.

The boys had been cleaning the downtown workplace for seven weeks. It closed at four each day, so they could begin their work just after school. Their earnings furnished extra cash for clothes and pastimes.

To amuse themselves, the boys thought about the people who worked in the rooms.

"This lady has so many pictures of pets on her desk," Leroy noted, "I bet she lives alone."

Jason stopped to survey someone's walls.

"This lady has so many pictures of pets on her desk," Leroy noted, "I bet she lives alone."

"This man seems like a real dreamer," he claimed. "His walls are filled with travel posters. He must hate working at a desk all day."

"Here is the strange one," Leroy pointed out. He stopped to comment on a desktop that was always tidy. "No pictures, no poems, no signs of life at all. You wouldn't even know a person worked at this desk."

"Very odd," Jason had to admit.

A Scribbled Note

When Jason and Leroy were cleaning a few weeks later, they saw something funny. The desk that had always been tidy was now a complete mess. It was littered with scraps of food and empty paper cups.

"Does the same person still sit here?" Leroy asked, looking for the name plate. "He must be nervous about something."

"Look at this," Jason said. He had knelt down to pick up a crumpled note on the floor.

Leroy could barely read the scribbled words.

"Look at this," Jason said.

"Classic Gifts best bet. Pretend to shop for silver bracelet. Noon Friday, April 20. Tell driver."

"Are you thinking what I'm thinking?" Jason turned to quiz Leroy.

"No wonder this man is restless!" Leroy blurted out. "He's planning to rob a store!"

A Pledge to Help

"What should we do?" Jason asked his buddy. "We can't ignore this."

"We have to inform the cops," Leroy urged. "I know one who will help us. She's chummy with my parents."

"Here," Jason said, handing Leroy a pencil. "Write the man's name on the note. The name plate says 'Robert Bellows.' "

"Got it!" Leroy stated as he slipped the note in his pocket. "Now we just have to locate Janet."

Leroy knew Janet often ate dinner at Kay's Diner on Willow Street.

The boys caught a subway that quickly took them there.

Leroy had made a good guess. Janet was sitting in a corner booth by herself. Her face beamed when she spotted Leroy.

"Well, this is a real honor," Janet spoke up. "Come join me."

"We need your help,"

Janet was sitting in a corner booth by herself.

Leroy began. "We found this note on the floor of a room we clean." He handed her the folded paper.

Janet read the note to herself. Then she looked squarely at Leroy. "I'll look into this," she pledged. "You did the correct thing."

Right on Schedule

By the time April 20 arrived, Jason and Leroy could hardly contain themselves. They were eager to know what would happen at Classic Gifts.

"We need to let Janet deal with this," Leroy

stressed. "But maybe we could observe." The boys knew the store stood on the corner of Valley and Haven Streets.

"That shouldn't be a problem," Jason spoke up. "We could sit in that nearby sandwich shop. To look normal, we could even order something."

So just before noon,

Jason and Leroy were sipping sodas in the sandwich shop near Classic Gifts. They sat at the main window, a perfect place to see any action.

Right on schedule, a plain white truck parked by the curb, but the driver stayed in his seat. The truck concealed the store's entrance, making it easy for a robber to enter and exit freely.

Within seconds, a cop car drove up behind the truck. Janet stepped out and quickly headed for the driver's window. She and the driver talked, surveyed the truck's contents, and then shook hands.

Shamed

As Janet turned to leave, she saw Jason and Leroy with their noses pressed to the sandwich shop window.

"Checking up on me?" Janet joked as she grabbed a chair at their table.

As Janet turned to leave, she saw Jason and Leroy with their noses pressed to the sandwich shop window.

"Maybe," said Leroy, leaning forward. "So what did you learn?"

"I learned the note you found concerned the filming of a TV ad, not the planning of a crime."

The boys looked confused. "But why the sudden change in Mr. Bellows' desk?" they asked.

"The work of an ad agent can be very stressful at times," Janet claimed. "He was likely feeling nervous."

The boys hung their heads.

"Listen," Janet went on. "We had to check this out." She paused to stress her next point. "But sometimes our daydreams can get the better of us. Just be aware of that." But Janet didn't think the boys had heard her.

Almost Famous

By the time the boys left the sandwich shop, a crowd of people was standing outside Classic Gifts. Inside, crewmen were setting up lights and photo gear. The boys eased in closer to observe.

“Hey, you two!” a well dressed man waved to them. “Want to be in our ad? We need some extras.”

Leroy and Jason perked up. “Are you kidding?” Leroy blurted. “Who wouldn’t!”

“What do we have to do?” Jason quickly asked.

“We need a few more shoppers to make the store

look crowded," the man told the boys. "I'll have the costume person help you."

"This is too cool!" Leroy shouted. "We're going to be on TV!"

"This could be the start of something really big," Jason added. "We could be famous someday."

High Frequency Words

are	been	come
could	do	does
from	have	into
lives	of	one
only	read	said
should	some	the
their	there	to
too	two	very
went	was	were
what	who	would
your		